To Elizabeth, Happy Birthday !! xx
YOU ARE

STARTING BALLET

Helen Edom and Nicola Katrak

(Nicola Katrak is artist in education with The Birmingham Royal Ballet.)

Designed by Maria Wheatley

Illustrated by Norman Young

Contents

About ballet

Classical ballet is an exciting way of dancing which began hundreds of years ago. The dancers' movements can show a mood or tell a story. This book tells you about ballet and shows you how to try out some first shapes and movements.

These dancers are a prince and princess in a ballet called The Sleeping Beauty.

Dancers make interesting shapes with their bodies, arms and legs.

A woman who dances the main part in a ballet is often called a ballerina.

Dancers' legs are usually turned outward like this.

Ballet dancers make pointed shapes with their feet.

It takes years of training to make shapes like this.

This kind of dress is called a tutu. It has a very short skirt so the dancer can move her legs easily.

You can watch a ballet live on stage, or on a film or video. The dancers move to music, often spinning very fast or jumping high into the air. Sometimes they pause to balance in wonderful shapes. Dancers train hard so they are strong and supple enough to do lots of different movements.

Ways of dancing

There are all sorts of ways to dance. You can make up your own movements if you like. But for many ways of dancing, like ballet, you learn to use special movements.

Tap dancers learn to tap out a rhythm with metal-tipped shoes.

In classical Indian dancing, each hand movement has a meaning so it helps to tell a story.

Finding a class

You need to find a class right from the beginning so a teacher can help you to learn. Look for advertisements for ballet classes* in your local newspaper or library.

*See page 32.

What to wear for ballet

Wear clothes that you can move easily in, such as leggings or shorts. You must be able to point your feet so wear soft shoes or, best of all, no shoes at all.

Tie your hair up out of the way.

Later on, if you like ballet, you can buy special dance clothes such as a leotard, tights, and ballet shoes. Ask your teacher before you decide what to buy.

Ballet shoes

You can buy ballet shoes from many shoe shops. They have soft soles so you can point your feet easily. Dancers sew on ribbons to keep them on their feet but it's easiest to start with elastic.

3

Dancing shapes

Dancers use lots of different movements and shapes to make a dance exciting to watch. See how many different shapes you can make with your body.

A wide, stretched shape.

This tall shape looks proud.

Strong arms help this shape to look fierce.

A small, round shape.

How many parts of your body can you make into a round shape? Think what you can do with your arms, back and fingers.

What shape would your body make if you had to fit into a small box? How much room can you take up if you really stretch?

See how many shapes you can think of that make you look frightening or proud. Stay still in each shape for a few seconds.

Moving shapes

Try moving with a rounded back.

Your arms and legs tuck in when you roll.

You can stretch your body up as you skip.

Your legs stretch out as you slide.

Now try moving. See how many different ways you can find to move across the room.

You could start from a rounded shape and try rolling, pouncing, crawling or creeping.

Then start from a stretched shape and try whirling, sliding, skipping or jumping.

Moving to music

In ballet, like most dancing, the movements are made to music. Listen to some music you like. How does it make you feel? Is it sad or happy, calm or angry?

Energetic jumps might go with exciting music.

Dragging steps could go with slow, sad music.

Hops and skips could go with cheerful music.

Think of ways you can move to suit the mood of the music. Remember to change the movements as the music changes mood.

Shapes to spot

Here are some shapes ballet dancers make. You may spot them when you see a performance.

This stretched shape is called an arabesque (say ara-besk).

This more rounded shape is called an attitude (say atty-tood).

Keeping in time

Dancers' movements often match the beat of the music.

Listen to some music with a strong beat. Try to clap or stamp in time with the music.

Try clapping your hands against a friend's. Listen carefully to the music so you do not get faster and faster.

5

Making a good start

It is easier to dance well, if you start from a good, straight position.

Ways of standing

People often stand with curved backs and rounded shoulders. Dancers pull up their bodies so they are as tall and straight as possible.

You might stand crookedly like this while waiting for a bus.

Look straight ahead of you.

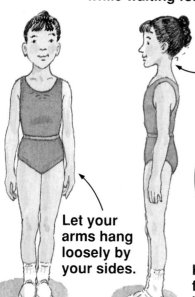

Let your arms hang loosely by your sides.

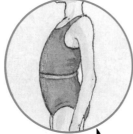

Keep your back flat, not curved like this.

Try standing like a dancer. Stand up tall with your feet together and your arms by your sides. Pull your tummy up to help you grow even taller.

Foot positions

For ballet, you need to start with your legs turned out. Here are three different starting positions to try.

Bring both heels together and turn out your legs so that your toes point outward. This is called the first position.

Your legs are turned out from the top.

Your feet make a V-shape.

Now put your feet apart like this. Keep your legs turned out. This is called the second position.

Keep your body and legs pulled up.

Stand firmly on both feet.

Then put one heel half way along the other foot. This is the third position. You can do this with either foot in front.

Turning out

Ballet dancers move with their legs turned outward. This helps them to lift their legs higher. Try this experiment to see how much difference turning out makes.

Arms turned in.

Arms turned out.

First, put the backs of your hands on the sides of your legs. Without twisting your arms, see how high you can lift them up to each side.

Then turn out your arms out so the palms face front. Now you can raise them as high as you like.

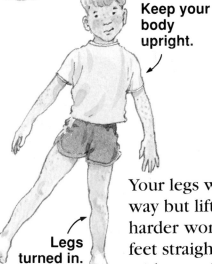

Keep your body upright.

Legs turned out.

Legs turned in.

Your legs work the same way but lifting them is harder work. Try with your feet straight and then try with your feet turned out.

Positions to spot

After a lot of training to help them turn out their legs, ballet dancers are able to use two more positions. See how often you notice them when you watch ballet.

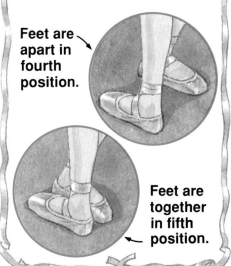

Feet are apart in fourth position.

Feet are together in fifth position.

High lifts

Dancers train for years so their legs become strong and turned out enough to make shapes like this.

First movements

The first movements in a ballet class help to make your muscles warm and stretchy. You often start off with some leg bends called demi-pliés (say demee-plee-aze). Demi-plié is a French name which means a half-bend.

Look straight ahead while you do this.

Keep both feet flat on the floor.

Start off with your feet in a V-shaped first position like this. Stand up as tall as you can and put your hands on your waist.

Slowly and smoothly bend your knees so they go outward over your toes. Then straighten your legs to stand up tall again.

Now try a demi-plié starting with your feet apart in second position. Remember to go down and up very smoothly.

Using the barre

Barre

Your arms are slightly bent.

Rest your hands lightly on the barre like this.

Trying at home

Your barre should be about waist-height.

Many dance rooms have a rail called a barre on the wall. You can hold this to help your balance.

There may be a mirror behind the barre. This helps you to check that your body is straight.

You can use the back of a steady chair or a table instead of a barre when you do ballet at home.

Body bends

Try another
bending
movement,
this time for
your back.

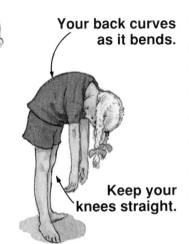

Your back curves as it bends.

Your arms hang loosely by your sides.

Keep your knees straight.

Start by standing up tall
with your legs in first
position. Let your head
feel heavy and very
gently drop it forward.

Now gently bend your
whole body forward,
following your head.
Let your arms flop
down toward the floor.

Some people can bend far enough to touch the floor.

Keep your feet flat on the floor in first position.

Bend over only as far as
feels comfortable. The
more times you do this,
the more easily you will
be able to bend.

Straighten up slowly
and smoothly so your
head comes up last of
all. Keep your legs tall
and straight all the time.

French names

Ballet movements have
French names because
ballet steps were first
written down in France
about 350
years ago.

**A French
dancer in the
eighteenth
century.**

**Dancers's shoes
used to have
heels like this.**

Dance training

Professional ballet dancers
go to classes every day to
make their muscles supple
and strong. They always
begin with pliés.

Moving your arms

In ballet, the way you move your arms is just as important as the way you move your legs.

Straight and curved

Your arms go straight when you reach for something.

Your elbows make sharp, pointed shapes when you dig.

Your arms can make all sorts of different shapes. How many can you think of?

When you use your arms in ballet, you often make round or softly curved shapes like this.

Shapes and movements

Try these arm shapes. Start by standing up tall with your arms by your sides.

Then lift your arms up in a smooth curve to make a circle in front of your tummy. This is called first position.

Try not to hunch your shoulders.

Let your fingers curve as well.

Keep your arms in the circle shape and raise them smoothly until they are almost above your head. This is called fifth position.

Let your eyes follow your hands as you move them.

Then open your arms out as if you were drawing a curve on each side of you. This is called second position.

Your arms are still gently curved.

See how smoothly you can move from first to fifth to second position. Always begin and finish with your arms by your sides.

10

Mixed positions

You can swap your arms and try these positions the other way around.

You can hold one arm in first position and one in second. This mixture is called third position.

Fourth position is another mixture. You hold one arm in fifth position and the other in second.

Arm waves

Gently press the air away with the back of your hand as your arm goes up.

Push the air away with your palm as your arm comes down.

Your arm is soft, not stiff.

Try this kneeling or standing.

See if you can make your arms move like birds' wings. Wave them up and down as smoothly as if you were underwater.

Swan Lake

In the ballet, Swan Lake, a princess has been magically changed into a swan. She moves her arms to make them look like swans' wings.

The dancer moves her neck like a swan.

Her head tilts so she can keep looking at her hand.

Her arms are always gently curved.

Pointing your feet

Ballet dancers point their feet so they can move smoothly and lightly. Try these exercises to help you point your feet.

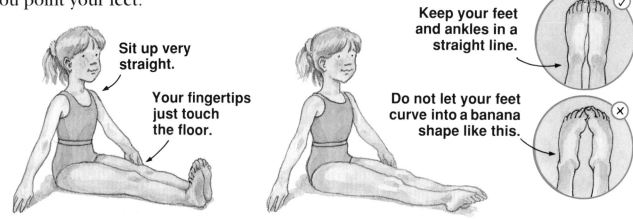

Sit up very straight.

Your fingertips just touch the floor.

Keep your feet and ankles in a straight line.

Do not let your feet curve into a banana shape like this.

First, sit on the floor with your legs straight in front of you. Bend your ankles so your toes point up to the ceiling.

Now slowly point your toes as far down to the ground as you can. The more you do this, the easier it becomes.

Trotting with pointed feet

Lift up your heel before your toes.

Point your toes as you lift them.

On the way down your toes touch the ground first.

As you get faster you can lift your feet higher.

Now stand up tall with your feet together. See if you can point your toes while you lift up one foot at a time. Hold onto a barre if you feel wobbly. Try this slowly at first, then get faster so you look like a pony trotting on the spot.

Quiet movements

Your movements become lighter and quieter when you point your feet. See how quietly you can skip with pointed toes.

You could use your quiet, pointed toes to pretend to creep into a secret place.

Swing your arms as you march.

Try marching or walking with pointed feet to see how lightly you can move.

Sliding and pointing

Dancers strengthen their feet with movements called battements tendus (say bat-mon-tohn-doos). They slide their feet to the back, side or front. This is how to do a battement tendu to the front.

Pull your body up as tall as you can.

First, stand up tall with your feet in first position and put your hands on your waist.

Your feet make a V-shape in first position.

Slide one foot forward firmly as if it is polishing the floor.

Your leg is always straight.

Point your toe while you count to three. Then slide your foot back to first position.

Imagine that your toes are making a tiny toeprint, not a big splotch.

Keep both legs turned out all the time.

Your toes never leave the ground.

13

Rising and balancing

Once you have started to stand up tall like a dancer (see page 6), you can learn to rise up on your toes and balance. In ballet, this is called standing on demi-pointe (say demee-point), or half-toe.

Pulling up

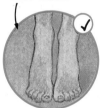

Start with your feet together, making yourself as tall as you can. Make your legs long and stretched too. Then try to grow even taller. Breathe in and rise on your toes.

It's easier to keep your balance if you look straight ahead.

Keep all your toes firmly on the ground like this.

Make your feet straight not banana-shaped.

Slowly lower your heels to the ground, keeping your body and legs as tall as you can. Now try rising up with your feet in first position. Remember to come down with your feet in the V-shape.

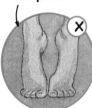

First position on demi-pointe.

Dancing on pointe

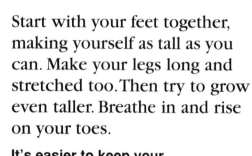

Ballerinas often dance on the very tips of their toes. This is called dancing on full pointe. It takes two years of training before a dancer's feet and legs are strong enough to even start pointe work.

This shows the ballerina's foot inside the shoe.

If you try this before you are about eleven, you will hurt yourself because the bones in your feet are still soft at the ends.

Pointe shoes

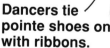

Ballerinas wear shoes with strong soles to help them go on pointe. The satin around the toes is stiffened with glue but there is no block inside.

Dancers tie pointe shoes on with ribbons.

Balancing on one leg

Dancers often balance on one leg to make ballet shapes. You can try balancing on one leg to make a shape called a retiré (say ret-earay). It is hard to balance like this so rest both hands on a barre, or a chair.

This foot stays flat on the floor.

Keep your body straight to help you balance.

Point your foot all the time.

Your toes fit into a hollow at the front of your knee.

Stand up tall in first position. Point one foot and put the toes on your other ankle.

Slide your toes smoothly up the side of your leg. Keep both legs turned out so your knee is sideways.

Stop still when your toes are by your knee. Now let go of your barre. How long can you balance?

Test your balance

Dancers need good balance. Try to stand on one foot on demi-pointe. Can you stay still without wobbling?

Make any shape that helps you balance.

Balancing on pointe

Ballerinas learn to balance on one leg while they are on pointe.

Male dancers hardly ever dance on full pointe but you can see them balancing on demi-pointe.

A retiré position on pointe.

This dancer's leg is stretched out in an arabesque.

Stretching your legs

Ballet dancers move their legs lightly and smoothly. They stretch their legs out straight, even when they are lifting them high into the air. Stretch your legs and point your toes when you try out these ballet movements.

Sliding out

Feet in first position

Push your foot strongly so you hear a swishing noise.

Your toes point as you slide them out.

Dancers do battements glissés like this to the side, back and front.

Your toes are only just above the ground.

Keep your knee straight.

This battement glissé (say bat-mon-glee-say) starts like a tendu (see page 13) to the side. From first position, slide one foot out sideways.

As soon as your toes are fully pointed, stretch your leg even more so your toes just leave the floor.

Then lower your pointed toes to the floor and slide your foot back to first position. Try this with your other leg.

Going faster

When professional dancers train, they do battements glissés very fast. They can do about 60 every minute.

Going higher

Try to keep your body still.

Leg out to the side.

Leg out to the front.

Lean forward when you throw your leg behind.

Now try throwing your leg higher after sliding it out. Then lower it smoothly to the floor.

This is a grand (say gron) battement. You can try this movement to the back and front as well.

A first arabesque

Keep your eyes still to help you balance.

Your front arm is stretched out in front of your nose.

Stretch this arm out low to the side.

There is a long line from front finger to back toe.

When dancers stretch one leg in the air behind them, they make a shape called an arabesque (say ara-besk). See if you can copy this one.

More arabesques

In ballet, you often see arabesques with the arms in different positions.

An arabesque with the arms this way around is called a second arabesque.

An arabesque with both arms in front is called a third arabesque.

Ballerinas may balance on pointe.

Gallop steps

Strong, stretched legs will help you to make bouncy gallop steps. Start by swinging your right leg to the side, then step onto it.

This is easier to do than it looks.

Swing your leg out.

Stretch your legs as much as you can.

This boy is moving from left to right.

Hop off this leg.

Point your toes.

Bend this leg as you land

Hop up from your right foot and close your legs in mid-air. Land on your left foot and swing your right leg out again.

Keep going, bouncing as high as you can with each step. You can go the other way if you swing out the left leg first.

Jumping

Whenever you jump, you have to bend your legs before you can spring up. See how high you go if you crouch down and spring up like a frog.

Your legs are very bent like this.

Straighten your legs as you spring up.

Pouncing like a cat.

You could also try pouncing like a cat. How far can you travel through the air?

Jumping from a demi-plié

Keep your body straight and tall.

Demi-plié

First position

Point your feet and straighten your legs.

Open your legs in mid-air to land in second position.

Second position

When you jump in ballet you keep your back straight when you bend your legs. Start in first position and bend both knees in a demi-plié*. Jump up and land in a quiet demi-plié. This sort of jump is called a sauté (say so-tay). Now start a sauté in first position and land in second position.

18   *See page 8.

Flying jumps

Dancers can stretch both legs out like this.

Ballet training makes a dancer's legs strong and stretchy. This helps dancers to jump very high.

Jumping on one leg

In some ballet steps, you jump from one foot to the other. This is called a petit jeté (say pet-ee jetay).

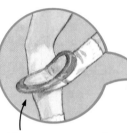

Your toes are just behind your calf

Bend your leg as you land.

First stand on one leg. Put your other foot behind your calf. Spring up and swap over so you land on the other leg. How many times can you do this?

Grand jeté

Try a travelling jump called a grand jeté (say gron-jetay). This means a big leap. You need lots of space.

Try to make stretched arm shapes.

Look up as you jump.

Stretch out your legs while they are in the air.

Bend your leg as you land.

Run with your legs and arms stretched out to help you take long strides. Make one stride into a jump by taking off from one foot and landing on the other.

19

Turning

Ballet dancers spin and whirl in many exciting ways. Here are some turns you can try.

Turning in the air

You can turn as you jump. In ballet, this is called tour en l'air (say toor-on-lair). Try turning around, jumping a quarter of the way at a time.

Lots of turns

Dancers always begin and end a tour en l'air (see left) with a demi-plié.

Some dancers jump so high they can turn around two or even three times while they are in the air.

Demi-plié in first position.

Bend your knees in a demi-plié as you land.

Around in one go

See if you can jump halfway, and then all the way around in one jump.

The higher you jump, the further you can turn.

Start from a demi-plié in first position. Jump up and turn a quarter so you can land in first position facing to the side. The next quarter-turns make you face the back, then the other side and then the front again.

Spinning and twirling

See how many ways you can find to turn quickly without jumping. How fast can you go?

Use your arms to help you get around.

You can move your feet in tiny steps or twirl on one leg.

If you spin for long, you get dizzy. Ballet dancers have a trick to stop them from getting dizzy. They keep looking at the same spot as they turn.

Pirouettes

Ballet dancers often spin around on one leg. This is called a pirouette (say pir-oo-et).

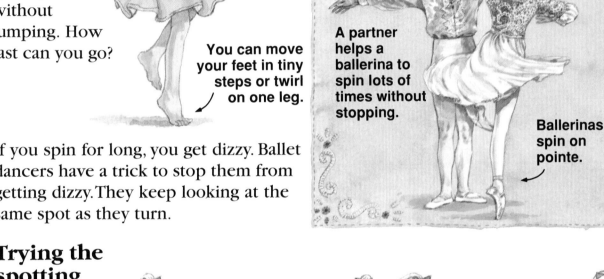

A partner helps a ballerina to spin lots of times without stopping.

Ballerinas spin on pointe.

Trying the spotting trick

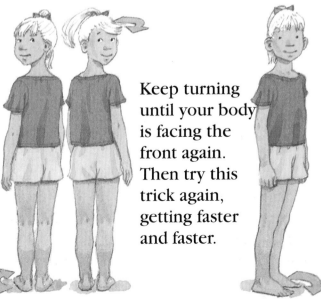

First look at a spot straight ahead. Keep looking at the same spot and do tiny steps to make a slow turn.

When you can no longer keep your eyes on your spot, whip your head quickly around to find your spot again.

Keep turning until your body is facing the front again. Then try this trick again, getting faster and faster.

Dancing together

In many ballets, groups of people dance exactly the same movements together. These groups are called the corps de ballet (say cor-de-balay).

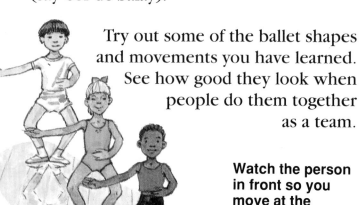

Try out some of the ballet shapes and movements you have learned. See how good they look when people do them together as a team.

Watch the person in front so you move at the same time.

The corps de ballet also make group patterns on the floor, like this curved line.

How many floor patterns can you make with your friends? Try standing in a straight line or making a triangle or circle shape.

There are many different ways of dancing with other people. In folk dancing, rows of people often line up and dance the movements together. Ballroom dancers usually dance facing each other in pairs.

Dancers may hold onto one another.

One ballroom dancer moves backward as the other moves forward.

A triangle shape

22

Dancing in pairs

Face your friend and ask her to do her own slow movements. Copy her exactly as if you are her reflection in the mirror.

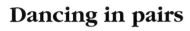

See if you can find ways to help a friend to jump higher. You have to find exactly the right moment to push up as he jumps.

Try standing behind your friend.

Can you do a petit jeté (see page 19) at exactly the same time?

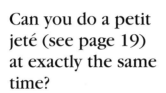

Instead of copying each other's movements, you could help each other to balance in interesting shapes.

It's easier to balance on one leg if you hold onto a partner.

These shapes make good beginnings and endings to a dance.

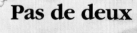

Pas de deux

In ballet, a man and a woman often dance in a pair. This is called a pas de deux (say pa-de-de). He helps her to balance and spin faster. He may even lift her high in the air.

Characters

Dancers play many different characters in ballet stories. Since they don't speak, their movements must show what sort of people they are.

See if you can turn yourself into a different person. You could be a rich prince, a wicked wizard or a fierce animal. Or you can be someone who is very funny, happy, cold or angry.

What shape might an old person make with her back?

Think how a spy might move his feet.

Find a way of moving for your character, then freeze in a still shape. What would your character do with his hands, head and body?

How can a wizard make a jump look evil?

Think of ways to prowl like a lion.

Try this with lots of other characters. Think of different movements for each one.

Costumes in ballet

Dancers' clothes give clues to show what characters they are playing.

This prince's costume is embroidered with gold to show how rich he is.

This dancer is dressed as a country girl.

Dancers in the ballet Les Sylphides wear floating white dresses with wings to show that they are spirits.

Dressing up

You could find costumes to help show different characters. They must be easy to move in.

You can make swirling movements with a cloak.

Use dark cloth for a witch's cloak. You could stick on stars and moons cut out of shiny paper.

Wrap tinsel around a hairband to make a princess's crown.

Dance with a ribbon tied to your wrist.

You could safety-pin tinsel to your dress.

Use face-paints to paint your nose red.

A funny character could wear clothes that are much too big. Ask if you can sew or stick on patches.

Masks

Sometimes dancers wear masks to show their characters. They have to be specially made so they are light enough to dance in and so the dancer can see out.

This mask helps the dancer to become a cat in the ballet, The Sleeping Beauty.

Make your own masks

You could stick shapes on top of your mask to make a head-dress.

Make big eye holes so you can see out.

Cut out a gap for your nose.

You can cut a paper plate into a mask shape. Paint it or stick on bright paper. Staple on ribbons so you can tie on the mask. You need practice to dance with it on.

Without words

In classical ballet, dancers never speak but they can use signs to help to tell a story. Using signs instead of words is called mime. Here is some mime you may see in a ballet.

Pushing hands out like this means "no".

Hand on heart means "like" or "love".

This means "me".

Pointing to an eye means "see".

A hand to the ear means "hear".

Mime puzzle

You can make up sentences with mime signs. Can you tell what this girl is trying to say? (The answer is at the bottom of page 27.)

Thanking

You can use this sign to thank your teacher after a class or an audience after a performance. It is called a revérence (say rev-air-ronce).

Hold out your hand to the person you are thanking and drop your head for a few seconds.

Bow your head as you bend your knees.

Girls may also take one leg behind the other and bend both knees in a curtsy.

Pretend party

Try making up a party scene with your friends. Instead of talking, use the mime signs on the left and make up some other signs of your own. This is even more fun to music.

Smile and wave to say "hello".

Your hands show how big your present is.

You can use signs to say "hello" to your friends, to give and receive presents and to ask for a drink.

Show how carefully you can pour a drink.

Try making up happy dance steps to show that everyone is having a good time.

Parties in ballets

Parties are a good excuse for lots of people to dance together. Look for party scenes in ballets. You can see a Christmas party in The Nutcracker, a grand ball in Swan Lake and a birthday party in The Sleeping Beauty.

Guests dance in The Nutcracker.

Puzzle answer: 'Please, you be quiet!' 27

Putting on a performance

Lots of different people work together to put on a ballet performance. Together they are called a ballet company.

Making up a ballet

Marks show the position of the dancers' legs and arms.

A choreographer chooses the music for a new ballet and makes the movements to go with it. These can be written down in signs like this.

Designing the ballet

A designer thinks up ideas for scenery. A model stage shows how the scenery will look. A lighting designer tries out different ways of lighting the stage on the model.

Then artists paint the full-size scenery onto huge sheets of canvas. Rocks and other things are made of polystyrene or papier mâché.

Costumes

The designer also draws ideas for the costumes. A wardrobe team makes all the costumes so they look like the drawings.

A principal dancer

Rehearsals

The dancers rehearse, or repeat, the steps many times to music. A few days before the performance, they begin to rehearse in the costumes on the stage. These are called dress rehearsals.

Make-up

The dancers wear thick make-up so their faces show up under the bright stage lights. They put this on just before a dress rehearsal or a performance.

Wings

Corps de ballet

The performance

The dancers warm up their muscles first so they do not hurt themselves when they dance. They wait at the side of the stage, called the wings, for their turn to go on.

Dancers dip their shoes in a powder called rosin to keep them from slipping on the stage.

When they are on stage, the dancers make their movements look light and easy so the audience will enjoy the performance.

A hidden orchestra plays the music in an orchestra pit.

Famous ballets

Ballets often tell magical stories, like fairytales. Here are the stories of some of the most famous ballets.

Coppélia

Franz and Swanilda are sweethearts until Franz falls in love with Coppélia. He thinks she is the daughter of Doctor Coppélius, a toy-maker.

Swanilda's friends help her to break into Doctor Coppélius' workshop. She discovers that Coppélia is only a doll and hides in a cupboard when Coppélius comes in.

Swanilda dressed as Coppélia.

Coppélius catches Franz sneaking into the workshop and drugs him. Coppélius then tries magic to put Franz's life into the doll.

Meanwhile Swanilda has dressed up in the doll's clothes. She dances to trick Coppélius into thinking he has really made Coppélia come alive. She runs off laughing with Franz when Coppélius realizes his mistake.

Swan Lake

Von Rothbart's evil spell forces princess Odette to change into a swan each day. One night, while Odette is in woman's shape, Prince Siegfried finds her by the lake and falls in love. If only he is faithful, his love can break the spell.

Odette

Prince

But Von Rothbart tricks Siegfried into being unfaithful by disguising his daughter Odile to look like Odette.

Odette wears a tutu decorated with swan feathers.

Odile's part is danced by the same ballerina who plays Odette.

Too late, Siegfried realizes his mistake and rushes off to find the real Odette. Now the spell can never be broken and the lovers decide to die together.

La Fille Mal Gardée

Lise and Colas

In La Fille Mal Gardée (say lah-fee-mal-guard-ay) Widow Simone wants her daughter Lise to marry Alain, the clumsy son of a rich farmer. But Lise is already in love with a young farmer called Colas.

After lots of lively scenes, including a real pony on stage and a clog dance, Lise and Colas finally outwit Simone so they can marry each other. The ballet ends with Lise and Colas dancing joyfully with their friends.

The Nutcracker

The nut-cracker doll

On Christmas Eve a little girl, Clara, is given a doll-shaped nutcracker. At midnight it turns into a prince who fights an army of rats.

Sugar Plum Fairy

Nutcracker Prince

Clara throws her slipper at the rat-king and the prince takes her across the Land of Snow to the Kingdom of Sweets. There Clara sees dances from different countries and the Sugar Plum Fairy dances a pas de deux with the prince. In the end Clara wakes to find that it was all a dream.

Index

Finding out more

You can write to these addresses to help you find a good ballet class.

Royal Academy of Dancing,
36 Battersea Square,
London, SW11 3RA, **UK**.

Royal Academy of Dancing,
250 W. 90th Str, 3a,
NY 10024, **USA**.

Royal Academy of Dancing,
20 Farrel Ave,
Darlinghurst,
NSW 2010, **Australia**.

Royal Academy of Dancing,
404/3284 Younge Street,
Toronto, Ontario,
M4N 2L6, **Canada**.

Royal Academy of Dancing,
British Cars Building,
19 Tory Street,
Wellington, **New Zealand**.

School visits

Many ballet companies hold workshops in schools. Ask your teacher to find out if a ballet company can visit your school.

Usborne Publishing would like to thank the following for use of photographs for artistic reference: Zoe Dominic, pages 2, 27 (bottom right), 30 (top right and bottom right), 31 (top and bottom right), Catherine Ashmore, page 30 (left), use of Anthony Crickmay photograph from the collections of the Theatre Museum by courtesy of the Board of Trustees of the Victoria and Albert Museum, page 7 (bottom right). Thanks also to children from the Royal Ballet's Chance to Dance programme and from Torriano Junior School who demonstrated the positions in this book.

First published in 1992 by Usborne Publishing Ltd, Usborne House, 83-85 Saffron Hill, London, EC1N 8RT, England. Copyright © 1992 Usborne Publishing Ltd.

Printed in Belgium.   First published in America March 1993